CONTENTS

GW00746452

LittleBrother BOOKS

Little Brother Books Ltd, Ground Floor,
23 Southernhay East, Exeter, Devon, EX1 1QL
books@littlebrotherbooks.co.uk | www.littlebrotherbooks.co.uk

The Little Brother Books trademarks, logos, email and website addresses and the Pop Winners logo and imprint are sole and exclusive properties of Little Brother Books Limited.
Published 202X. Printed in China.
Little Brother Boots, 77 Camden Street Lower, Dublin D02 XE80.

WELCOME TO THE WORLD OF ROBLOX!

Whether you're a noob or a pro, there's something for everyone within the pages of this ultimate GamesWarrior Roblox guide. You'll find out everything you need to know about your favourite games, discover fun new experiences and learn all sorts of amazing Roblox facts!

The GamesWarrior team reveals everything you need to know get you started in Roblox, the different types of experiences to try out, the best games players have been trying in 2024, the coolest skins to pick up and much, much more.

Also, be sure to check out which reader's avatars impressed the GamesWarrior team on pages 22-25.

GAMESWARRIOR SAYS

Once you've read through the whole book, be sure to try your hand at the Ultimate Roblox Quiz on pages 32-33 to find out just how much you know!

ROBLOX YEAR IN REVIEW

It's been a busy year in the world of Roblox, with all kinds of new experiences, content and in-game events. Here's a look back over the last 12 months and all of the cool stuff that's happened!

US store Walmart added its own experience to Roblox this year, one that lets players over the age of 13 order items from within the game and have them delivered!

PvP Skullbeat is one of many Roblox games that's made it out of beta testing and can now be experienced. The rhythm game is already proving to be a massive hit!

Fan favourite manga character Doraemon entered the Roblox universe in March 2024. Players can check out Doraemon Nobita's Go-Go Ride right now.

The Hunt: First Edition metaverse event took place in early 2024, with 100 different Roblox titles involved. Players had to find over 100 hidden badges, exciting cosmetic rewards, infinite eggs and much more!

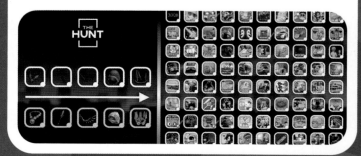

GAMESWARRIOR SAYS

Did you know there are now more than 40 million different gaming experiences available to play on Roblox?

It's now possible to play Roblox in VR on Meta Quest! Players can immerse themselves in their favourite experiences like never before, with 3D worlds coming to life, right in front of their eyes.

Supercar fans can now check out the Lamborghini Lanzador in Roblox, taking a virtual drive in the manufacturer's all-electric Ultra GT years before it hits the streets for real.

Sportswear brand adidas is now in Roblox, with virtual pop-up stores selling wearable items for your avatar, plus a limited edition adidas x Rush X Pack available for free!

Pop superstar Nicki Manaj celebrated the launch of her new album, Pink Friday 2, with a surprise Roblox experience. Fans were able to explore her 3D shop and buy all kinds of exclusive items!

GAMESWARRIOR SAYS

The NBA joined Roblox last year, with NBA Playgrounds offering 1-on-1 and 2-on-2 basketball games, complete with official shirts!

BEST ROBLOX GAMES OF 2024

You'll find all kinds of amazing Roblox experiences in this GamesWarrior guide. To give you a preview of what's to come in the book, check out the best games of 2024 here!

RPG: DUNGEON QUEST

PAGE 20

One of the best and biggest Roblox RPGs to date, Dungeon Quest includes multiple dungeons, combat and multiplayer action.

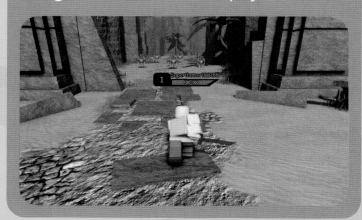

ANIME: BLOX FRUITS

PAGE 30

Explore all kinds of strange islands, battle tough enemies and collect lots of different fruit in Blox Fruits, a Roblox game that's been visited over 32 billion times!

OBBY: TOWER OF HELL

PAGE 40

A tough and testing Obby experience, Tower of Hell pushes players to the limit and beyond, with plenty of challenging levels requiring some serious skill.

ADVENTURE: ROYALE HIGH

PAGE 46

Royale High continues to be a massively popular Roblox game with players from all over the world who want to try out this fantasy adventure!

TYCOON: RESTAURANT TYCOON 2

A smash hit Roblox experience, Restaurant Tycoon 2 is a test of players' business skills as they try to keep customers happy with tasty food.

SIMULATOR: ADOPT ME!

Probably the biggest Roblox game available, Adopt Me! allows players to raise a variety of pets, furnish their home, buy vehicles and much more!

FIGHTING: THE STRONGEST BATTLEGROUNDS

Step into the arena and prepare to take on tough opponents in a PvP fighting game that requires skill, stamina, timing and the will to survive.

SURVIVAL: NATURAL DISASTER SURVIVAL

Who knew disasters could be so much fun? In Natural Disaster Survival, you'll battle against the elements themselves to see how you can stay alive and in one piece!

SPORTS: SUPER STRIKER LEAGUE

Whether playing solo or in a team with your friends, Super Strike League offers the ultimate Roblox sports game, one that you'll keep coming back to time and again.

CREATING AN ACCOUNT AND AVATAR

Before you can get started, you'll need to create your own Roblox account and avatar. GamesWarrior has checked out how to do both, so let's find out how easy it is!

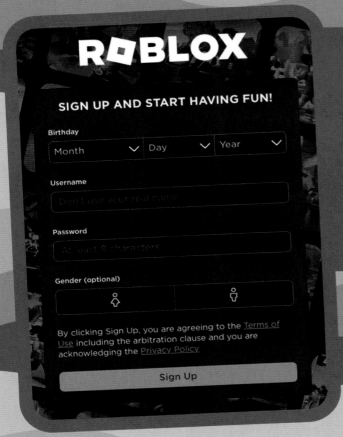

To begin playing Roblox, you'll need a video game console, a Mac or a PC and access to internet broadband, so check with whoever pays the bill first.

Creating a new Roblox account is really quick and easy. Just download the game to your device or head to the Roblox homepage on your Mac or PC.

Now fill in the required details (don't use your real name though) and be sure to make a note of your password in case you ever log out of the game.

GAMESWARRIOR SAYS

When you successfully verify your Roblox account you'll get a bonus free item, like this cool hat!

Thank You!

Your email has been verified. Enjoy the free hat!

View Item

You may be asked to verify your account with an email address or mobile number. Make sure you get permission from a parent or guardian first before you do so!

Avatar Editor

Explore the marketplace to find more clothes! **Get More**

Recent ⌄ **Characters** ⌄ **Clothing** ⌄ **Accessories** ⌄ **Head & Body** ⌄ **Animations** ⌄

Recent › All

| Pal Hair | Verified, Bonafide, | Rthro Climb | Rthro Fall | Rthro Idle | Rthro Jump |

| Rthro Run | Rthro Swim | Rthro Walk | Man Head | Man Torso | Man Right Arm |

| Man Left Arm | Man Left Leg | Man Right Leg | Smile | Man Face | Brown Hair |

3D

Body Type   0%

Avatar isn't loading correctly?
                    Redraw

You're almost ready to play! All you need to do now is make an avatar – a virtual version of you that will appear in most Roblox games.

Players start off with a very basic avatar, but we think it's really fun to then customise your character with all kinds of body types, faces, clothing and animations.

If you want to change your avatar, we recommend using items in your inventory or heading to the Marketplace for free stuff to buy with your Robux (see page 12).

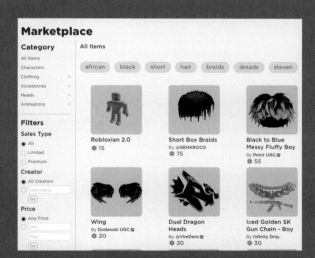

Players have tons of fun messing around with the Avatar Editor. See what kind of crazy looks you can come up with before starting your own Roblox journey!

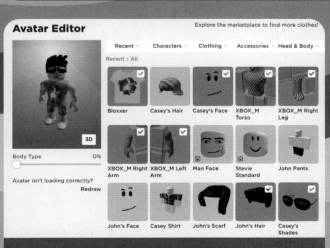

GAMESWARRIOR SAYS

You can keep track of your account on your one player Profile page. Add in some text to let other players know who you are and what you like.

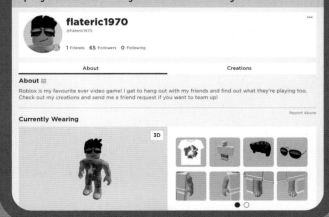

11

ROBUX AND MARKETPLACE

If you want to take your Roblox gaming to the next level, you'll definitely need some Robux! This virtual currency can be bought with real money and allows players to purchase awesome digital in-game items and extras.

BUYING ROBUX

In the UK, 400 Robux currently costs £4.99. However, if you choose a monthly Robux subscription that's then boosted to 450 Robux!

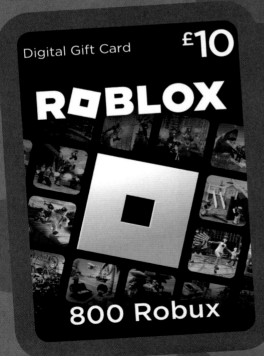

GIFT CARDS

As well as being able to buy Robux in the game itself, you can also get physical Roblox Gift Cards. These can range in price from as little as £10, right up to a whopping £200. Roblox Gift Cards also come with exclusive virtual items, such as some awesome special outfits!

READY TO SPEND

Now that you've got some Robux, head over to the Marketplace in the main game menu to find out what you can purchase with them. There are all sorts of cool items to splash your cash on, from clothing and accessories to avatar heads and even animations.

MARKETPLACE

Items in the Marketplace are arranged in different categories and you can even filter your search to look for certain genres such as sports, RPGs and sci-fi. Once you've purchased an item, it will then be added to your inventory ready for you to use.

LIMITED
Despacitegg
◎ 124

LIMITED
Goldrow
◎ 111

LIMITED
Eggmunition
◎ 140

LIMITED
Party Unicorn
Floatie
◎ 160

LIMITED
Rocket Eggscape
◎ 115

LIMITED
Fried Chicken
Egg
◎ 110

LIMITED
Black Iron
Branches
◎ 480

LIMITED
Tiny Tank Egg
◎ 119

Shark Backpack
By Rey x Noob
◎ 20

Robloxian 2.0
◎ 15

Wing
By Dodanuki UGC
◎ 20

red tactical
sunglasses
By @WhoseTrade
◎ 55

Shiny Teeth
◎ 35

Black Twisted
Dreadlocks
By TYPE 9
◎ 65

Messy Fluffy
Anime Boy Hair
By @viorz
◎ 65

Pro Sword
Fighter Chain -
By Bow and Arrow St...
◎ 20

CatNap
By Tyler and Snow!
◎ 65

☑CatNap☑
By Totkisha 3D Studio
◎ 90

FREE STUFF

If you're ever short of Robux, head to the Marketplace and check out the many free items that are available. We recommend grabbing as much stuff as you can when you first start gaming, allowing you to play around with the look of your avatar!

ROBUX PREMIUM

Robux Premium is a paid-for subscription service that comes with all kinds of tempting perks. For starters, you'll get Robux gifted to you each and every month and even gain access to special items that are unavailable to other players.

Roblox Premium
Get Premium

PREMIUM MEMBERS

Robux Premium members are also able to trade items in the game and earn Robux from selling stuff. You can then use any Robux you make to buy even more amazing things in the marketplace!

+10%

More Robux
Get 10% more when you buy Robux

Trade
Unlock the ability to trade items

GAMESWARRIOR SAYS

You can always treat your friends and family to a Robux Gift Card, as they make for perfect birthday treats! We think the best way to buy Robux though is through a monthly subscription, but all of the free items available in the Marketplace are also worth adding to your inventory too.

WARNING: ALWAYS ASK PERMISSION BEFORE BUYING ANYTHING ONLINE! NOTE THAT YOU CAN'T OFFICIALLY EARN FREE ROBUX IN GAMES. THERE ARE A LOT OF SCAMMERS OUT THERE THAT SAY THEY'RE GIVING AWAY FREE ROBUX - THESE ARE BEST AVOIDED ALTOGETHER!

ROBLOX EXPERIENCES

There are lots of different Roblox experiences (or games) to try out and players usually have their favourites. However, it's always worth trying new experiences to see if you like them, such as any of the games in this book!

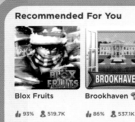

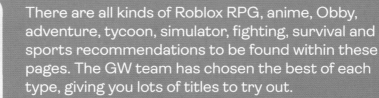

There are all kinds of Roblox RPG, anime, Obby, adventure, tycoon, simulator, fighting, survival and sports recommendations to be found within these pages. The GW team has chosen the best of each type, giving you lots of titles to try out.

Some players like to start off with slightly easier games that they can get to grips with, before moving on to more complicated Roblox experiences. This is a really good strategy, as everyone learns to master different games at their own pace.

When you start playing Roblox, you'll be able to use the search bar at the top to find the games you're looking for. Roblox will also recommend different types of experiences to try out, such as by clicking the Discover link at the top of the screen.

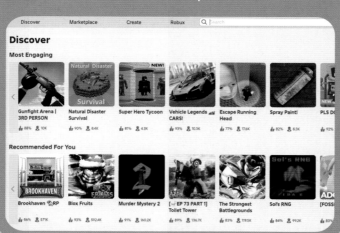

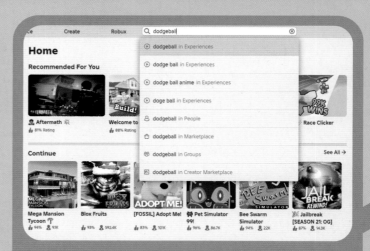

This selection can include Most Engaging, Exclusive Subscription Benefits, Up-and-Coming, Popular, Top-Rated and many more. You can also see what games other players are trying out, which is a good way to be inspired by other titles.

Some players who really like a Roblox game click on the Groups option and join other members to chat about their favourite experiences!

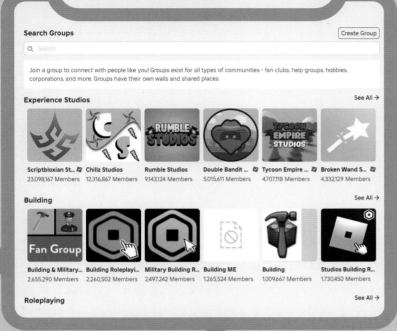

New Roblox players tend to try Obby or adventure games first to get used to those experiences before then moving onto new games. Others like playing whatever games their friends are currently playing, sometimes joining them online.

That's a really good idea if you've not played Roblox before, as working together as part of a team can really help you learn how to master a game. Once you're ready, you'll then be able to tackle an experience on your own and quickly level up!

RPGs, tycoon, simulator and survival experiences can be challenging for some players who may not be used to grinding to level up. That means spending a lot of time with a game, slowly improving your character by learning about the world you're in.

One of the great things about Roblox is that new games are being added all the time. In addition, most of the existing Roblox games get regular updates and extra content, meaning there's always something fresh to discover or try out!

Some Roblox games can fit into more than one category, such as Basketball Pro Simulator being both a great sports and simulator experience!

RPG GAMING STRATEGIES

If you've never tackled an RPG (role-playing game) before, or are just looking to boost your skills, then GamesWarrior has you covered with expert reviews of all the latest gaming strategies to get the most out of your fantasy adventures.

You'll need to have plenty of patience when it comes to playing RPGs, as you often have to put in a lot of grind to really get anywhere. The best RPG players take their time, exploring every area for items to level up and unlock new powers and weapons.

Some enemies can be really tough and almost impossible to beat on your own. That's why RPGs are best experienced as part of group, with a team of adventurers being harder to beat, especially when it comes to all-powerful bosses.

Winning gamers choose the right class for their characters at the very start of a game. Whether it's a sword-swinging warrior or a magic-using mage, it can make a really big difference in the epic battles to come.

One simple strategy players rely on to enhance their character and gaming experience is to check out the stores in RPGs. Shopkeepers sell and buy a wide variety of items, weapons, armour and other extras that can come in very handy.

GAMESWARRIOR SAYS

Perhaps the easiest strategy that mindful players use is to never forget to pick up gold or coins from their defeated enemies!

RPG SIMULATOR

Millions of players around the world have already tried RPG Simulator. This awesome Roblox game features an epic adventure that can be tackled on your own or in a party of friends. Get ready for some full-on fantasy questing!

It's pretty easy for players to quickly level up in RPG Simulator and they can do so by either conquering the game's zones or by completing challenging raids. Players will also be rewarded with loot for buying items and even pets.

The Max Level in the game is 1,401, but it'll definitely take you a long time to achieve that! Pro players start by exploring each of the various zones and tackling smaller monsters, before heading off to take on tougher quests and bosses.

It's possible to have up to 16 players taking part in RPG Simulator at the same time. Players who stick together when tackling larger foes can preserve more of their energy, so there's definitely strength in numbers.

In addition to weapons, RPG Simulator allows players to learn a variety of special skills that can help them out in battles. Those skills can then be enhanced by finding jewelled rune stones to further power yourself up.

GAMESWARRIOR VERDICT

If you're new to the world of MMORPGs, then RPG Simulator is definitely well-worth checking out. You'll soon learn how to take down foes and team up with other adventurers and being part of a group makes the game more enjoyable and playable!

GW RATING ★★★★★

SWORDBURST 2

If you're looking for one of the best Roblox RPGs available, then Swordburst 2 may be just what you're after! This popular multiplayer titles is inspired by the Sword Art Online anime and is the sequel to Swordburst Online.

In Swordburst 2, players have to join forces and travel across an expansive open-world to defeat enemies and collect items. That may sound simple enough, but there are all sorts of obstacles and dangers to face along the way!

Swordburst 2 contains all-new areas to discover every time you enter the world, but you'll only be able to unlock them once you beat a tough boss. Wise players know it's best to team up with their friends or other players to tackle these stages.

Each player is equipped with their own special sword that's designed to take down specific enemies and other weapons for close combat. Defeat your enemies to earn more cash and then buy better gear to beat bigger foes. Simple!

There's quite a bit of grinding in Swordburst 2, which can mean you often have to put in a lot of effort to really get anywhere. However, players who do stick with the game will be rewarded with an RPG that has plenty of longevity.

GAMESWARRIOR VERDICT

Swordburst 2 takes a little while to get into, but it's worth investing the time. The grind can be a bit repetitive though, so you'll need to stick with the game to make any real progress. Players will discover this is one RPG that's worth sticking with!

GW RATING ★★★★☆

WORLD // ZERO

One of the best-looking and biggest Roblox MMORPGs out there, World // Zero is an epic adventure just waiting to be experienced. Trek through a variety of worlds, battle fearsome enemies and complete challenging quests!

There are over 30 unique dungeons to tackle across 10 open-worlds in World // Zero. You'll need to take down challenging foes and defeat big bosses in order to level up. Doing so unlocks new classes and quests, so it's well worth it!

Another aspect of World // Zero that players enjoy are its pets. You can choose from a selection of friendly critters to join you on your RPG adventure and there are over 50 different pets that can be added to your collection.

World // Zero is really fun when playing with your mates and you'll definitely need to team up in order to take down some of the game's tougher bosses. You'll be glad you did though, as you'll soon level up and be rewarded with lots of loot!

GAMESWARRIOR VERDICT

World // Zero is easily one of the best Roblox RPGs out there and it continues to get better all the time. There's just so much for players to see and do in the game that you'll definitely be coming back to challenge it time and again.

GW RATING ★★★★★

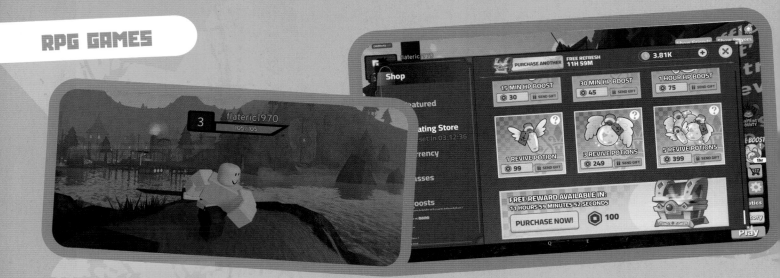

DUNGEON QUEST

With two billion visits to date, it's no wonder that Dungeon Quest is the most popular Roblox RPG! The MMORPG has been around since 2018, but continues to grow in size, with exciting new content being added all of the time.

Sure, players can always tackle Dungeon Quest on their own, but it's much more fun when you team up with other adventurers! There are currently 16 unique dungeons to tackle, multiple warrior classes to unlock and many rare items to be found.

Dungeon Quest players get rewarded with armour, weapons, abilities and cosmetics. They can also get skills points when they level up, gain gold for purchasing stuff and buy all sorts of handy item upgrades too.

Dungeon Quest offers up Daily Rewards for regular players, which many think is a great way to get free items and more gold. However, what you get depends on the level you're currently at, so players try to improve their skills to earn better goodies!

The Mobs (or enemies) in Dungeon Quest can range from easily-defeated Sand Peasants to super-tough bosses. One strategy some players use to earn more gold and level up to the max is to defeat every foe that they encounter.

Dungeon Quest features regular in-game events that can score you big prizes. For instance, the 2024 Easter event included a lobby egg hunt, a special battlepass, new Boost types in the store and the Bunny King boss raid!

Speaking of the Dungeon Quest store, this is the place to visit if you're looking for extras to help you improve your gaming experience. Players can pick up handy enchantments for their weapons, 2X gold, VIP bonuses and much more.

Another great feature most players like to try out in Dungeon Quest is the RPG's trading system. This lets you exchange up to 14 items from your inventory with other players, which many find a useful way to get hold of seriously rare stuff.

From the Desert Temple to Pirate Island, Dungeon Quest's levels boast different challenges for players of all skill levels. One strategy real pro players use is to tackle Dungeon Quest's Nightmare mode to try and earn Legendary weapons!

GAMESWARRIOR VERDICT

Dungeon Quest continues to be the biggest and best Roblox RPG experience out there and it's a title millions just can't stop playing. Whether you try solo or team up with others, this is a fantasy gaming experience that really is like no other!

RATING

LET'S HEAR FROM OUR READERS

We've had hundreds of readers write to us to share their avatars. Here are some of GamesWarrior's top 20 favourites!

Alfie – Age 8

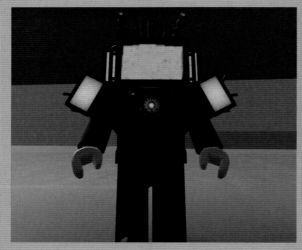

Check out Alfie's awesome outfit with a TV screen for a head!

Carlo – Age 12

The wings on this avatar are huge and we like the rainbow top too.

Charlotte – Age 8

How cute is Charlotte's outfit? Frog-themed glasses as well!

Conor – Age 8

Who needs a human face when you can have a cool cat head instead?

Drew – Age 13

Drew's gone for orange as a main outfit colour and it looks cool.

Frazer – Age 6

We don't know about you, but we wouldn't pick a fight with this guy!

Freddie – Age 6

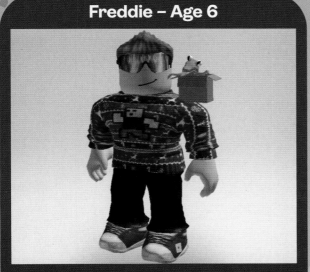

Take a look at Freddie's great design for an outfit with pet combo.

George – Age 8

Wow! George's avatar has a totally unique two-tone outfit.

Harry – Age 7

When it comes to street smart outfits, this is one of the best!

Isabelle – Age 10

Isabelle impressed us with her pink outfit and star-shaped glasses.

Libby – Age 10

Libby's got great fashion sense, as this outfit clrearly shows!

Lucas – Age 12

There's nothing better than a smartly-dressed ninja.

Lydia – Age 8

Lydia is ready to party in this sparkly outfit for her avatar.

Maddison – Age 5

Check out Maddison's fantastic Roblox avatar outfit design!

Miguel –Age 11

We're giving Miguel a big GW thumbs-up for this creation.

Niall – Age 10

Niall has totally nailed the art of looking ultra cool!

Olivia – Age 8

Take a look at the colourful wings on Olivia's stunning outfit!

Oscar – Age 7

Oscar's impressive blue outfit almost leaps of the page.

Sienna – Age 10

We suspect we know exactly what Sienna's favourite animal might be.

Sophia – Age 9

A funny Stitch head is the finishing touch for Sophia's outfit!

GAMESWARRIOR SAYS

CONGRATULATIONS TO ALL THE AMAZING READERS WHOSE AVATARS ARE FEATURED ON THESE PAGES! KEEP UP THE FANTASTIC WORK!

YOU'RE ALL ROBLOX SUPERSTARS!

ANIME GAMING STRATEGIES

B$ 320
SuperGamer100155

B$32
Bandit
-20.77

If you're a big fan of all things anime and manga, then you're in luck! There are all kinds of amazing Roblox games based around your favourite shows, films and characters, each of which offers up a different play experience.

A lot of anime games follow the same route as fighting and RPG titles, so players will often find themselves spending a lot of time grinding to try and level up. This is a good thing to do though, as it's the best way to get new abilities and weapons!

A lot of anime game players have discovered that it's better to take on an adventure or battle as part of a larger group. While solo play can be fun, powerful enemies and bosses can be dispatched much faster when teaming up with others.

One strategy that some players employ is to check out a game's store to see what extras are available. Items may cost in-game currency or even precious Robux, but can often really help you make it through tough battles and onto the next.

Another reason why plenty of Roblox players enjoy playing anime games is because of their favourite characters. Famous faces from the likes of Dragonball Z, One Piece, Bleach, Naruto and Demon Slayer can all be found in various titles.

QUEST
Head Jailer

Rare
Lv.2 Double plunger
636/1.1K

Rare
Lv.2 Double plunger
604/1.1K

GAMESWARRIOR FACT

If you're an anime fan, then Roblox has you covered. You'll find all sorts of different anime games to get to grips with, from solo adventures to massive multiplayer brawls – there's something for almost everyone!

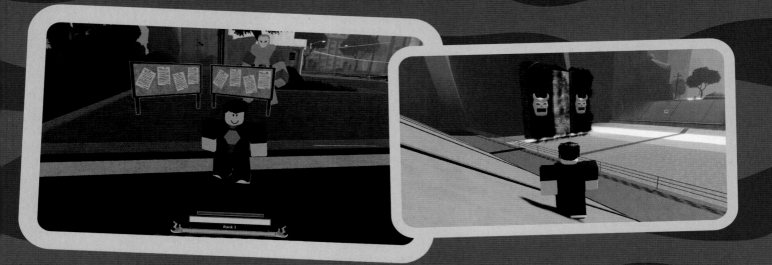

SOUL WAR

Although updates have now stopped for Soul War, it's still a satisfying Roblox anime game that's worth checking out. The goal is for players to defeat the soul invaders and destroy the gates, while defending their own castle.

If a team of heroes manages to survive until round 6 and beat it, they'll then get a shot at fighting the mini-boss, WEEGEE. Once defeated, they then have to try and take down the creator of the game and evil versions of other players!

One reason that a lot of players enjoy spending time with Soul War is that there are lots of different weapons to find and unlock. These can range from close-up melee weapons such as the Soul Edge blade and Bat, to the Medigun and Flamethrower.

The game also includes Soul Classes, with some tough enemies requiring at least five or six people to team up and destroy them. That's why many players prefer to tackle the game in groups, as strength in numbers is the only way to survive!

The best players try to level up their characters by taking on various quests. Doing so then grants their characters special skill points, which can be used to unlock even more new abilities and bonuses on the skill tree.

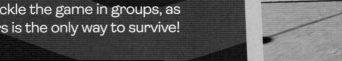

GAMESWARRIOR VERDICT

Soul War is a really different kind of anime game, one that encourages teamwork in order to be successful. There are plenty of rewards and new skills to obtain, with the ability to level up your character resulting in some truly epic battles!

GW RATING ★★★★☆

ANIME SWORD SIMULATOR

As with many similar Roblox games, Anime Sword Simulator brings together a variety of anime characters in one place to battle it out and see who's the winner. The main aim of the game is to level up your character and unlock different swords.

Most of the weapons are unique and easy to get and can be obtained by taking down enemies. Once you've defeated your foes, your character is then rewarded with their special sword to add to your ever-growing collection of weapons.

Top players take their time to hone their fighting skills, reaching levels where they're strong enough to survive almost any skirmish. As you become stronger, you'll unlock even more amazing abilities that will really assist you in later battles.

There's definitely plenty to do in Anime Sword Simulator, with lots of new worlds to explore, pets to collect, unique challenges to beat and all kinds of swords to obtain. Some players also like opening eggs with coins to unlock Strong Heroes!

GAMESWARRIOR VERDICT

With large islands to explore and fast-paced battles to survive, Anime Sword Simulator is definitely a massive hit with players. As with other Roblox games, the more grind you put in, the more amazing rewards and achievements you'll receive.

A ONE PIECE GAME

Based on the massive Japanese manga series created by Eiichiro Oda, A One Piece Game is a massive Roblox hit that was launched by Boss Studios in 2022. There are lots of different islands to explore, quests to complete and enemies to battle!

Some players might not like the amount of grinding there is to do in the game, but it's essential to put some time in to get the most out of it. Those that do are rewarded with new skills that they can then use to take on tough boss raids.

Each of the islands in the game is huge and takes a lot of exploring. One strategy top players use is to tackle every enemy in one area to build up their abilities, before moving onto the next island to gain even more skills.

Tackling a One Piece game on your own is tons of fun, but most players find that the Roblox experience is better when teamed with friends. Big bosses are definitely much easier to defeat if you have a few powered-up mates by your side!

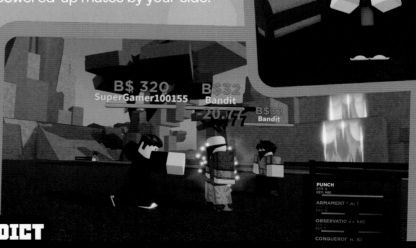

GAMESWARRIOR VERDICT

This is easily one of the best Roblox One Piece games available, with so much to see, do and unlock as you progress. Whether in solo mode or teaming up with others, you'll discover that A One Piece Game is a blast!

GW RATING ★ ★ ★ ★ ★

BLOX FRUITS

PICK A SIDE!

PIRATES   MARINES

Defy the marines and battle pirates!
Create your own pirate crew!
Get a high player bounty!

Team up on pirates
Faster, cheaper ship
Claim bounties

Fast Mode

Reduces LAG by disabling material
(recommended for Mobile)

If you're looking for the biggest and most popular anime game currently available on Roblox, then Blox Fruits is the clear winner. With over 32 billion views so far, this experience keeps attracting all kinds of players from around the world.

Blox Fruits is inspired by One Piece and gives players the chance to explore lots of different seas and islands. Gamers can choose to become a Blox Fruit 'devil fruit' user, gain special powers or become skilled with a variety of swords.

At the start of Blox Fruits, players have to choose from either Pirates or Marines as a faction. Beginners usually opt for Marines, as this strategy gives them 50% off buying ships later on, which can really come in handy.

Once you've chosen your side, players are then required to interact with NPCs for quests that help them earn money and XP to level up. Successfully completing each quest also gives gamers cash to spend on various items, upgrades and abilities.

Top Blox Fruits players will know that when you level up, you also get three skills points. These can then be used to boost your stats, improving Melee, Defense, Sword, Gun and Blox Fruit abilities.

Safe Zone - PvP disabled

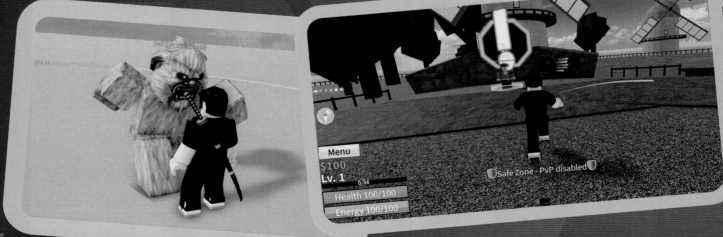

Menu

$100

Lv. 1   0/86

Health 100/100

Energy 100/100

Safe Zone - PvP disabled

The second island in the game is the Jungle, complete with monkeys and gorillas to fight. There is also a challenging boss on the island, but the best strategy that we've seen others use is to level up first before taking on this tough foe.

Eating Blox Fruits gives players really powerful abilities that depend on which fruit you've consumed. Pro players always avoid swimming after eating Blox Fruits, as your health will decrease if you do and your character will eventually die.

It's possible for players to level up both their weapons and abilities by defeating enemies and being rewarded with what their foe has. Those who have been playing Blox Fruits long enough also know that there are special codes available to boost XP.

GAMESWARRIOR VERDICT

With 39 different fruits to choose from, lots of different islands to explore and a wide variety of weapons and abilities, it's easy to see why Blox Fruits is such a popular game. This is definitely one Roblox experience that has to be played!

GW RATING ★★★★★

ULTIMATE ROBLOX QUIZ

Find out how much you know about Roblox by taking this ultimate quiz! All of the answers to the questions on these pages can be found within this book, so see how many you can get right.

1 Which 2024 metaverse event involved 100 different Roblox games?

2 What's the Max Level that you can reach in RPG Simulator?

3 How many visits has Speed Run 4 had to date?

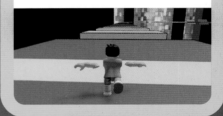

4 What's the maximum number of players that can take part in Hide and Seek Extreme?

5 Which Roblox game has added cute pet patients on its Sky Floor?

6 What's the name of the developer behind Bee Swarm Simulator?

7 What was the original title of The Strongest Battlegrounds?

8 Which survival game lets you unlock and play as a prehistoric Mosasaurus?

9 What are the names of the two coloured teams in Dodgeball!?

10

Which sportswear brand added virtual pop-up shops in Roblox in 2024?

11

What do you get when you verify your Roblox account?

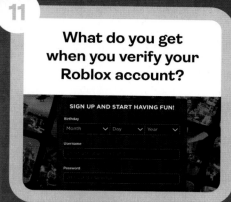

SIGN UP AND START HAVING FUN!

Birthday

Month ∨ Day ∨ Year ∨

Username

Password

12

What's the name of the Roblox paid-for subscription service?

13

Which Roblox RPG was inspired by the Sword Art Online anime?

14

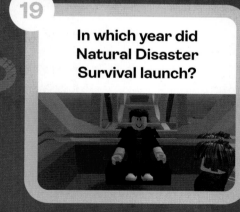

What's the name of the mini-boss in Soul War?

15

How many different stages are currently in Cotton Obby!?

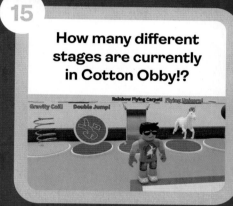

16

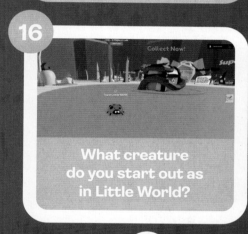

What creature do you start out as in Little World?

17

Which simulator game includes over 1,000 pets?

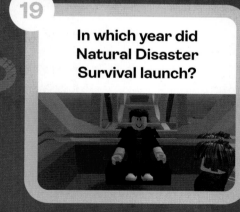

18

How many new skill moves can you unlock in Boxing League?

19

In which year did Natural Disaster Survival launch?

20

Which sports game lets you score a goal from the moon?

GAMESWARRIOR RATING

1-5: You're off to a great start, noob!
6-10: Wow, you really know your Roblox games.
11-15: Congrats on an amazing score.
16-20: Well done. You're a true Roblox pro!

COOLEST ROBLOX OUTFITS

There are all kinds of outfits to get in Roblox and you can even make your own if you like. Here's our rundown of the best outfits to get from the Marketplace.

HULK

It's possible for players to transform themselves into the Incredible Hulk for less than 100 Robux, making this a popular look with many Roblox gamers!

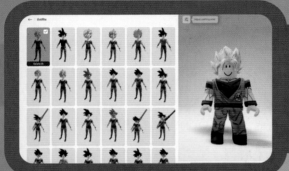

GOKU

This ultra-cool Dragonball Z outfit can be yours for just 85 Robux, transforming your avatar into the legendary Goku himself.

SANTA CLAUS

Here's a festive Roblox outfit that lots of players have purchased! Costing 95 Robux, this Santa Claus look also comes with a bushy white beard.

NINJA

Some players like to transform their avatars into stealthy ninjas for sneaking around in games and this great look will set you back 459 Robux.

GAMESWARRIOR SAYS

There are all kinds of free Roblox outfit items available from the Marketplace, so try some on to see which you like the best!

PRINCESS

Become a fairy tale princess by purchasing this outfit. It does cost quite a lot at 400 Robux though, but there are cheaper alternatives available.

DEMON

This striking red and black demon is a popular choice with many players. The 205 Robux outfit also comes with massive wings that look awesome!

ONE PIECE

There are lots of different One Piece character outfits available to purchase in Roblox, such as this Monkey D. Luffy skin for 290 Robux.

BATMAN

Become the Dark Knight by changing the look of your avatar to Batman. This outfit costs 248 Robux, but it's definitely one of the best superhero skins.

OBBY GAMING STRATEGIES

If you're a complete noob or even a real pro when it comes to playing Obby games, there's always something new to learn. GamesWarrior has reviewed the latest gaming strategies for mastering all kinds of Roblox parkour titles.

Most Obbys aren't a race, so you can really take your time and tackle each stage as slow or as fast as you like. While early levels might not be much of a challenge, you'll need to put in plenty of practise time to crack later stages.

The most savvy players regularly save their games so they don't loose any progress. This is particularly useful on much longer Obby levels and means you won't lose any progress if your internet connection happens to go down.

The most successful Obby players make sure to check their positioning before they make a jump. It can be risky to stand too close to the edge of an obstacle or ledge, as you can sometimes get hit by a nearby object.

It's also very easy to miss a jump. Top Obby players position their camera to make sure they are in the right place before they make a leap. Not knowing where you're jumping to is a sure-fire way to result in a respawn and lose precious time.

SPEED RUN 4

Players need to have lightning-fast reflexes and nerves of steel if they want beat this mega-popular Obby game. The goal is to make it through 30 different stages to reach the end and unlock crazy new dimensions!

There's plenty to like about Speed Run 4 and it's a game lots of players have spent time with. One of the great things about this Obby is that the levels start off pretty easy, but soon get harder the longer you stick with it.

As well as unlimited dimensions to unlock, Speed Run 4 also includes multiple challenges to beat after collecting stars and extra content to buy, if you have enough Robux. Complete a level and you get rewarded with gems to unlock even more stuff!

Speed Run 4 has had over 1.5 billion visits since it launched, so that should give you an idea of just how good it is. While playing on your own is tons of fun, most gamers find that the PvP races are a great way to see how their times compare with others.

Up to 30 players can be on a Speed Run 4 level at any given time. Watching the top players, you'll see how cracking some stages is second nature to them. So before you leap in, sit back and watch how others tackle a stage first!

GAMESWARRIOR VERDICT

Speed Run 4 is easily one of the best and most popular Obby games out there. Billions of players have spent hours leaping through its 30 levels before moving on to the new dimensions. Whether solo or with your friends, this game is a blast!

GW RATING ★★★★★

COTTON OBBY!

Prepare to enter a cotton-coloured world of parkour challenges with this really fun Obby game.

There are currently 55 different stages to test out your jumping skills on in Cotton Obby!, with each challenging level getting tougher the further you progress.

You can have up to 15 players competing against each other in Cotton Obby!, with some of the game's crazy stages being a complete mad dash to the finish line to beat your opponents.

Some players like to take their time tackling each course, but pros aim for accuracy over speed as a good way to play this game. There were plenty of times we thought we were going to win, but mistimed a leap and fell to our doom!

Smart players check out the Cotton Obby! store to grab awesome power-ups such as the Speed Coil, Gravity Coil or Rainbow Magic Carpet, as well as cute pets to join them on their epic speed runs. We found some of the extras can really help when tackling levels.

GAMESWARRIOR VERDICT

Cotton Obby! is a peaceful pastel game that's pretty fun to play on your own and even better with up to 15 friends! The levels can start to get quite tricky later on, so grab some power-ups from the store and get plenty of practise in before you tackle them.

RATING ★★★★★

MEGA EASY OBBY

Mega Easy Obby features a whopping 825 unique stages to tackle, with each one offering players a different level of challenge.

Walking along an invisible tightrope, dodging falling rocks, balancing on a rotating rainbow pathway and making your way through a maze of spinning lasers are just some of the 825 crazy stages players will encounter in Mega Easy Obby!

You can try to beat each level in solo play or invite your mates along to tackle courses. Up to 12 people can take part in Mega Easy Obby at once, which can result in some crazy sprints to the finish. Players who've beaten a course once often like to go back and try each level again to see if they can smash their overall best times!

Mega Easy Obby also rewards players with gems every time they successfully complete a level. These can then be used to buy all sorts of handy items in the shop, such as a Grapple Hook, Jetpack, Double Jump and Fusion Coil, which some gamers find very handy later on!

GAMESWARRIOR VERDICT

With a staggering number of stages, Mega Easy Obby is one of our favourite Obby games! We reckon playing with lots of friends is awesome, but being able to improve your times on levels is also great. Pro players take their time to make it through every challenging stage in one piece.

GW RATING ★★★★⯨

TOWER OF HELL

If it's a real Obby challenge you're after, then look no further. With over 22.9 billion visits to date, Tower of Hell is easily one of the most popular, testing and nail-biting Roblox games available. Are you ready? Then let's jump right in!

You may have tried lots of different Obby games, but Tower of Hell is a different beast altogether. Players have to compete against each to reach the top of a level first and there are no checkpoints available whatsoever!

That means you're going to not only have to keep an eye on all of the randomly-generated stages and obstacles it throws at you, but also be watching for other players taking advantage of any annoying mistakes you might make along the way.

Tower of Hell's difficulty level might be a little off-putting for new players, but those who practise on other Obby games will hone their skills faster. What's more, the title's time limit is another factor that adds plenty of pressure to tense races.

Up to 20 players can compete against others on each stage, which makes for some serious gaming sessions. The best players try to keep their cool to avoid making any wrong moves, ending back in last place or out of the action for good.

It's worth noting that Tower of Hell's stages reset every eight minutes and every player that finishes the level then speeds up the timer for everyone else. Top payers try to stay close to the front pack as much as possible to be in with a chance.

There are an incredible 345 sections to check out in Tower of Hell, as well as 25 secret sections. In addition, the Pro Towers definitely aren't for beginners, but do reward players with two more minutes and 2.5 times more coins for winning.

As well as a number of private servers, VIPs can set up their own servers and use the settings menu to skip rounds, set the size of the tower and lock the shop – which players think is a great way of offering up a variety of challenges.

If you're going to try out your Obby skills on Tower of Hell, then get ready for plenty of setbacks. The best players know it takes time to master this game, but when you do, victory tastes even sweeter!

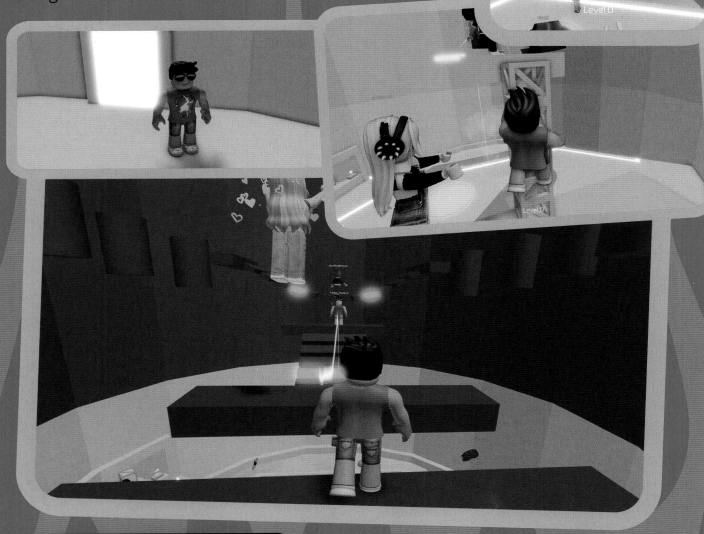

GAMESWARRIOR VERDICT

Tower of Hell can be punishing, annoying and frustrating to play, but it's also very satisfying when you complete a level. Don't let the game's difficulty setting put you off – there's a reason this title is in the top four Roblox games of all time!

RATING ★★★★★

ADVENTURE GAMING STRATEGIES

When it comes to Roblox adventure games, there are certainly plenty of great titles to choose from. Millions of players all over the globe have tried the experiences shown over the next few pages, so you should give them a go too!

A lot of adventure games include fun quests for players to take on. This is a good strategy, as it lets you learn all about the world you're in, what you have to do next and what level other players have managed to reach.

Exploring an adventure game on your own can be fun, but some players much prefer to tackle their adventures with others. Working together as a team allows you to progress further, take down big bosses and share in the rewards!

Learning how to level up in adventure games is essential if you want to keep improving. The top players take their time getting to know the world they are in, grind in battles to gain new skills and discover all they can about an adventure game.

Many Roblox adventure titles also contain mini-games, which you should try out. Those players who do often discover that they can unlock bonus items and extras, which can then be used to upgrade their character's abilities.

Press & hold behind the backs of police to pickpocket their keycard!

GAMESWARRIOR SAYS

If you try out lots of different adventure games, you'll soon work out which ones you prefer. Stick with those and become the best that you can at each experience and you'll soon become a true pro player!

LITTLE WORLD

Little World shrinks you down to a ladybug and you get to explore a tiny world of insects and plants! At that size, players have to battle various creatures, level up, grab new items and work together in order to survive the microscopic worlds.

Gamers start out as a cute little ladybug when they first begin their Little World adventure. Battles with other insects brings rewards, such as EXP and berries, plus there are flags to capture on each map, chests to locate and tough bosses to beat.

A big reason why Little World has been so successful is that there are currently a whopping 161 different bugs to unlock in the game! Players also enjoy taking part in quests to receive rewards and achievements, being part of a team and trying mini-games.

Fun new content is added to Little World all of the time, including more enemies and massive bosses. It's also possible for players to find and eat various fruit that can be found in each level, giving your bugs all sorts of abilities!

Seasoned pros take their time with Little World, trying out a variety of insects to see which they prefer and then levelling them up in battles. Having a wide selection of bugs with different skills is one really good way to come out on top!

GAMESWARRIOR VERDICT

With over 220 million visits since it launched in 2020, Little World is a smash hit Roblox experience. Players will find themselves revisiting the game on a regular basis to see what's new and team up with others to beat the toughest of bosses.

GW RATING ★★★★★

HIDE AND SEEK EXTREME

This Roblox experience takes a simple kids' game and turns it into one of the best Roblox titles out there! In Hide and Seek Extreme, one player is the seeker and has to find everyone else who is hiding somewhere in each level.

When a new games starts, one player is chosen to be 'It' and is given a special ability. Everyone else then has to run off and find a good spot to tuck themselves away in each of the giant-sized stages, hoping not to be discovered!

Up to 13 players can take part in a Hide and Seek Extreme session and when everyone has been found, a random gamer then becomes 'It'. That's one of the reasons why the Roblox experience is so popular with players and has lasted so long.

Some pro players are so good at Hide and Seek Extreme that they're almost never found before the timer runs out! The strategy most use is to choose a good first hiding spot, then keep an eye on the seeker and only move elsewhere when it's safe.

GAMESWARRIOR VERDICT

There's no denying just how much fun Hide and Seek Extreme is, whether you're doing the hiding or finding. You'll never know if your location is a good one or not until it's too late, which gives players a real thrill every single time!

RATING ★★★★★

JAILBREAK

One of the most famous Roblox games of all time, Jailbreak was created by developer Badimo and launched in 2017. Play as a criminal trying to escape from prison or a police officer trying to catch all of the convicts!

The award-winning Jailbreak can be played solo or as part of a team, with lots of gamers preferring to join forces in order to succeed. Inmates who manage to make it out of the prison then go on to perform robberies while being chased by the law!

One big reason why so many players enjoy Jailbreak is that the game play options are just so extensive. There are quests to undertake, vehicles to access, weapons and items to find and regular special events that keep the game fresh.

Another great thing players like about Jailbreak is that it's possible to switch teams during the game, from prisoners to police and back again. However, top gamers have soon discovered you can only do this after a few hours of playing.

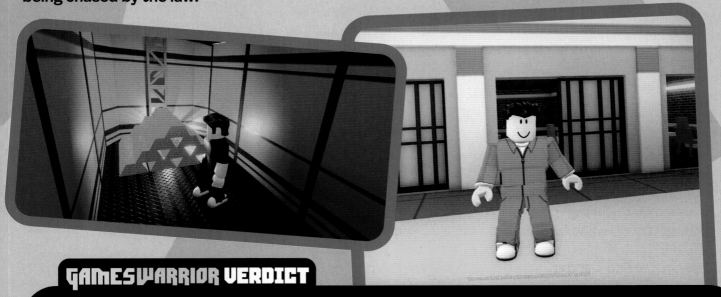

GAMESWARRIOR VERDICT

Jailbreak continues to be a massive hit, adding regular content to keep things interesting. This is one of the first Roblox games most players will try out and it's easy to see why it's still such a huge success after so many years.

RATING ★★★★★

ROYALE HIGH

Set across multiple fantasy worlds, Royale High is a magical Roblox title that features fairies, mermaids and other magical creatures. Enrol in high school, attend lessons and travel to various realms thanks to a handy teleportation system.

Millions of players have put in lots of hours with Royale High and it's easy to see why. There's just so much to find, do and experience in the game, that you'll definitely be spending many hours discovering everything the title has to offer.

The Teleport Map is used to access all of the other realms, instantly taking players from one colourful location to the next. There are also some special realms that can only be accessed during limited special events, such as Wickery Cliff for Halloween!

Players will soon discover that they can earn diamonds in Royale High, which are the game's currency. They can be obtained by doing quests, taking part in classes, levelling up, winning mini-games, finding chests and logging in every day.

Pro gamers know to check out the fountain every day to earn regular rewards and to progress the game's story. The fountain can always be found on the Main Campus, but sometimes pops up in other realms, and can be wished on every two hours.

Royale High has its own trading system too, which allows players to swap various items with each other. Exchanges can be made at the Intergalactic Trading Hub, although that feature is only available to those players at level 75 or above.

One of the main features of Royale High is the ability to level up your character. Doing so rewards gamers with diamond prizes, Sparkly Star achievements and access to some realms that would usually require them to be at a much higher level.

If you're already a big fan of Royale High, then Jazwares has all kinds of toys based on the game. Each collectible comes with various mix and match accessories, as well as a scratch-off panel that reveals a code for an exclusive virtual item!

GAMESWARRIOR VERDICT

Millions of players have already checked out Royale High and you should too. There are plenty of colourful realms to explore and achievements waiting to be unlocked, so be sure to head out on your own magical adventure today!

GW RATING ★★★★★

TYCOON GAMING STRATEGIES

Some Tycoon games can be a little confusing when you first start playing them, but there's no need to worry. One strategy some gamers try is to take things slowly to start off with, so you can get used to the play mechanics of each Roblox tycoon experience.

Top players try to earn as much cash as quickly as they can. That then allows them to buy more items to help their business grow, which in turn will bring in more money, allow them to level up faster and give them access to more stuff.

Any current valid free codes for tycoon titles can usually be found with a quick search online and we've included a few in this section of the book. Those handy extras can really make a difference early on in some challenging games!

When some players reach a certain level, they hang onto their money for a little longer and let it grow. When they've managed to bank a sizeable sum, they'll then be able to purchase those more expensive items that were previously out of reach.

GAMESWARRIOR SAYS

Always try a multiplayer version of a tycoon game to see what other players are doing and what kind of stuff they've bought!

HOSPITAL TYCOON

For a Roblox tycoon game with a difference, go check out Hospital Tycoon! The aim of the game is to run your own hospital, earning an income and using it add to your building, buy medical supplies and hire more staff.

As you progress through the game, you'll spend a lot of your time running over buttons to purchase all kinds of essentials. While some will cost you in-game cash, there are also a lot of premium purchases, which can be a bit annoying.

Pros build up their hospital as quickly as they can, using the cash they're constantly earning to get even better equipment, materials and workers. The game has also recently added cute pet patients on the Sky Floor, which are worth a look!

Keeping an eye on your patients is a good strategy, otherwise you won't make enough money to level up. Remember that the game is just as much about the people staying in the hospital as it is about running your own successful business.

GAMESWARRIOR VERDICT

The GW team definitely gives Hospital Tycoon a big thumbs-up as a Roblox experience you really should try. You'll have a massive and successful hospital up and running in no time, with lots of happy patients on every floor!

GW RATING ★★★★★

TROPICAL RESORT TYCOON

In Tropical Resort Tycoon, players are given a whole island and can use it to create their own holiday destination. That means you'll need to learn how to run a hotel, attractions and other areas, working very hard to keep customers happy!

One strategy some players use if to hire the hardest working employees they can to build up their resort as quickly as possible. If you do that then your guests will want to keep visiting and the cash will keep rolling in too.

Players have to start off with the basics though – don't expect to have a private helipad straight away! Those who take their time and slowly work up and enhance each area will soon have a very impressive holiday resort indeed.

Once players are ready to expand their island beyond the hotel complex, they can use various vehicles to explore the surroundings. These include buggies, boats and cars, as well as a helicopter for some fun aerial sightseeing!

In addition to swimming pools, a beach area and an airport, players can even add their own games for guests to play. One strategy is to include an Obby Island challenge, which is a great way to keep visitors occupied while you get on with more work!

GAMESWARRIOR VERDICT

Tropical Resort Tycoon is easily one of the best Roblox tycoon titles available so far and you'll definitely keep coming back for more. Start off slowly and you'll soon have an impressive holiday destination that all your mates will want to visit!

RATING ★★★★★

MEGA MANSION TYCOON

If you want to show off to your gaming friends, then Mega Mansion Tycoon is the Roblox experience for you! As the title says, players need to construct the biggest and most impressive mansion they can using money they collect.

Players earn cash every second based on how large their house is and can use their earnings to buy all kinds of cool stuff. That includes new sections to unlock, building materials, furniture, accessories, luxury vehicles and much more.

Most of the time you'll be playing Mega Mansion Tycoon solo, but there is also a multiplayer mode. Some players really like this option as they can then see how well other players are doing and compare their mansion to their own in-progress buildings.

You'll also notice lots of buttons on the floor in Mega Mansion Tycoon. When you run over those you'll be able to buy various items, if you have enough money. Some are premium items though and require paid-for Robux in order to get them.

GAMESWARRIOR VERDICT

Build a giant house, buy a flashy sports car and get paid big bucks - Mega Mansion Tycoon has it all! This is one Roblox tycoon game the GW team just can't stop playing and we think you'll go crazy for it too.

GW RATING ★★★★★

RESTAURANT TYCOON 2

If you feel like you've mastered the rest of the tycoon games in this section of the book, then get ready for a true challenge! Restaurant Tycoon 2 is slightly more complex than similar Roblox experiences, but we still think it's tons of fun.

For starters, you'll begin the game with a completely empty lot, but it'll soon get filled up. You can build up the area with upgrades to purchase, adding more floors to your restaurant and making the whole building much bigger.

Players then move onto the next stage, which is where they're able to customise the look of the place with different furniture and decorations. The top gamers start off by hiring staff, such as waiters and cooks, to deal with all the customers!

You don't have to just sit back and let everyone else do all the work though. In Restaurant Tycoon 2 you can pop into the kitchen yourself to cook up some tasty treats or even take part in some fun mini games while you're waiting around.

Restaurant Tycoon 2 is a really well-balanced game and you'll soon discover yourself levelling-up quite quickly. As you do so, you'll then be able to learn plenty of new recipes to make, which will attract lots of different kinds of people.

You don't have to wait around for long in Restaurant Tycoon 2 for anything to happen, as there's always something going on. Just wait until your business becomes really popular and you try to keep up with all of the customer demand!

Another thing players really like about Restaurant Tycoon 2 is the fact that you can invite your friends to dine at your eatery or even go and visit theirs. Some try different items on their menus and you can then add those to your own food selection.

One good strategy is to visit the Restaurant Tycoon 2 store. Inside you'll find a whole host of extras to enhance your gaming experience, such as Mega Tables, More Worker Slots, Auto Money Collection, 2 x Eating Speed and much more!

GAMESWARRIOR VERDICT

It's easy to see why Restaurant Tycoon 2 is a smash hit Roblox experience. There's so much to do and see in the game and you'll always feel like you're making progress. Go see what kind of top restaurateur you can become today!

GW RATING ★★★★★

SIMULATOR GAMING STRATEGIES

When it comes to being a master of Roblox simulator games, GamesWarrior has you covered. These type of experiences may be new to you, but follow these strategies and you'll soon be making the most out of even the toughest games!

Lots of top simulator players get to know how each game works first, as they can be very different, with specific rules to follow. We think putting in some quality time first is helpful to fully understand the different games and goals to aim for.

As soon as players start they try to level up as quickly as possible, in order to gain better items, abilities, moves and levels. This is a really good strategy to open up even more game play options.

Another strategy players use is to talk to others. They often give advice and even trade items. This can be a good idea once you've played enough of a simulator on your own. Who knows – they could even join you on your next quest!

Clever players will check out the in-game stores or shops for all kinds of useful items. As you progress, you'll usually collect some sort of currency that can be used to purchase extra items or abilities to enhance your character.

GAMESWARRIOR SAYS

Just like RPGs, here's usually a bit of grinding to be done in Roblox simulators before you can access the best stuff!

BEE SWARM SIMULATOR

Players are always buzzing around telling their friends just how much fun Bee Swarm Simulator is! In this great game you can grow your own swarm of bees, collect pollen, make lots of tasty honey, meet friendly bears and more.

By completing certain quests in this multiplayer experience, you'll get various rewards. Finish quests for bears, bees and even game developer Onett and you could bag yourself free honey, royal jelly and a silver egg!

The reason that lots of players love Bee Swarm Simulator is just how much exploring they can do in the game. As your hive grows larger, you'll be able to open up even more of the mountain and gain access to many all-new levels.

Thankfully, your bees aren't just for show and they'll come in really handy for completing quests. Guide the swarm to defeat dangerous bugs and monsters and be rewarded with all kinds of cool new items.

The best gamers always visit the in-game shops to buy better tools that can be upgraded with pollen. This is good for a quick fix, but be warned – some of them can cost a lot of honey!

GAMESWARRIOR VERDICT

With fun quests to complete and plenty to see and do, Bee Swarm Simulator is one of our favourite games. Developer Onett has crafted a very rewarding Roblox experience that we encourage you to get stuck into and then show your mates!

GW RATING ★★★★★

MINING SIMULATOR 2

Rumble Studios' Mining Simulator 2 is easily one of the best Roblox experiences of the year, one that many gamers have discovered is tons of fun either in solo mode or even better with a team of friends.

The aim of this game is to mine deep underground and strike it rich by digging up all kinds of rare gems. The more jewels you find, the better equipment you can buy, leading to more impressive gem discoveries!

One of the main reasons top players find Mining Simulator 2 so enjoyable is not knowing what they'll discover while excavating. The game also has lots of different levels to explore, pets and gear to unlock and so much more to experience.

Savvy players know to head to the game's store in order to spend their Robux on cool extras such as the Infinity Backpack and Teleporter.

Enhancing your backpack, gear, tools and pets as soon as you can is one strategy the best players use take to boost their mining abilites – which then helps them to gather extra resources for finding even more precious gems.

Mining Simulator 2 is really fun because the game gets all sorts of regular updates from its developer, Rumble Studios. Those can include new seasons, pets, items, secrets, ancients and so much more.

GAMESWARRIOR VERDICT

We think that Mining Simulator 2 is one of the better Roblox sequels available, with lots of new features to try out. Whether you're digging solo or teaming up as a squad, exploring underground has never been so much fun!

GW RATING ★★★★★

PET SIMULATOR X

The third game in this popular series, Pet Simulator X is a big upgrade on the first two Roblox experiences. However, this one is still all about collecting coins and gems, then using them to unlock even more powerful pets!

It's surprising how many coins players need, not only to hatch eggs but also for purchasing and accessing new biomes. Players will discover new worlds as they progress through the game, some of which have new features.

Players like the fact that there are so many different eggs to unlock in Pet Simulator X – even gold versions as well! With over 1,000 pets, it could take a while before you collect every one though.

Smart players keep an eye out for special seasonal events that can pop up. In the past, these have included themed pets for occasions such as Valentine's Day, Cinco de Mayo, St. Patrick's Day and many other holidays.

GAMESWARRIOR VERDICT

Pet Simulator X continues all the fun and excitement of collecting from previous games, but really takes it to the next level. This is one Roblox experience the GamesWarrior team really enjoys, so be sure to go check it out now.

GW RATING ★★★★☆

ADOPT ME!

So you want to play one of the most successful Roblox games of all time? Well, Adopt Me! has been visited a staggering 36 billion times, making it one of the biggest MMO titles ever. Get ready to care for and raise some of the cutest critters around...

Adopt Me! used to be all about being a child or a parent, but has shifted to looking after virtual pets. Different creatures hatch from eggs and can be collected and traded with other players.

The pets in Adopt Me! fit into one of five classes: Common, Uncommon, Rare, Ultra-Rare and Legendary. Four fully grown pets of the same type can be combined into a Neon pet and four Neons into a Mega-Neon!

There are two different ways to purchase pets in Adopt Me!, either by spending Robux or through the game's virtual currency, Bucks. Some players do find it a bit annoying though that they can't get certain expensive pets right away.

Earning Bucks is pretty easy, as you just have to keep your pet happy, feed and water it regularly, buy it toys and so on. You can also spend any Bucks you gain on pet accessories, buildings, potions, vehicles and furniture for your house.

The main appeal of Adopt Me! is the ability to build up a massive collection of virtual pets – once you have a few, you'll want more! Comparing your collection to other players' can also be fun, but don't get too jealous of what they may have.

Developer Uplift Games has added limited edition pets into the game over the last few years, which some players think is a great idea. That's included such surprise guests as Scooby-Doo, a Galaxy Explorer pet to promote Sing 2 and even a Zodiac Minion Chick!

Did you know there are Jazwares Adopt Me! toys that you can buy? They include playsets with figures and cuddly plushes, with the real-world items also bundled with extras such as virtual item codes for the game and an adoption certificate.

Uplift Games really supports its players, with regular updates and events being rolled out for Adopt Me! all the time. Many players think this is a really great idea, as it keeps the game fresh and makes them want to come visit Adopt Me! time and again.

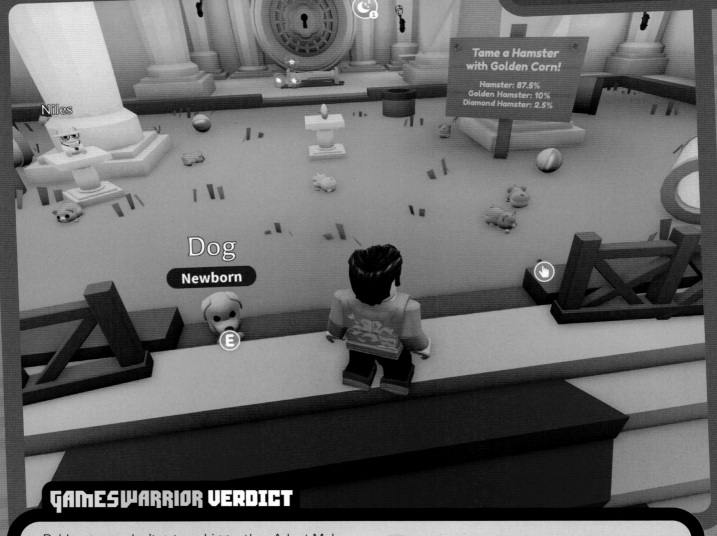

GAMESWARRIOR VERDICT

Roblox games don't get any bigger than Adopt Me! If you're looking for a really fun game to get stuck into that keeps you coming back, then this is the one. If you haven't already played it yet, go start your own awesome virtual pet collection today.

FIGHTING GAMING STRATEGIES

There are plenty of useful strategies that players use to survive in Roblox fighting games that you can learn too. While some may take a while to master, patience and practise is what makes the top gamers real pros.

One mistake that new players make is to keep attacking their opponents before they themselves run out of energy. That's why defence is actually more important, knowing when to block, parry and avoid an enemy's assault!

Another smart strategy to employ is to make sure you've levelled up before taking on really tough foes. Inexperienced players won't last long against an opponent who has much higher stats than them and the outcome is always their defeat.

Many pro players put a lot of hours into their favourite Roblox fighting games, so they really know them inside out. They can anticipate other gamers' moves in advance and which counters to use to take them down in record time!

As well as being able to enhance your character's abilities, lots of fighting games offer players upgrades for their equipment and even pets. The best players choose both wisely and ensure they also get levelled up to assist them in battles.

GAMESWARRIOR SAYS

Don't be put off fighting games if you lose a lot. True warriors are forged in the heart of battle and spend days mastering a new Roblox fighting title!

BOXING LEAGUE

Step into the ring, keep your guard up, keep your feet moving and get ready to be declared the champion in Boxing League! This Roblox fighter lets you build up your battling skill, take down tough opponents and learn all-new moves.

In Boxing League, players will get up close and personal with rivals, using a combination of multiple punches, jabs and swings, while keeping an eye on their defence and how much stamina they have left to survive each round.

A good strategy that more experienced players use is to choose the best counters to use against your opponent's attacks. Sometimes blocking is the answer, while other bouts require competitors to unleash a flurry of fast-paced hits!

As players progress through Boxing League, they'll level up and be able to unlock one of 14 new skill moves. You'll get to keep each new ability you gain and it's possible for fighters to combine them for some serious damage.

Inside the Smoll Gym, players are able to try out their moves before taking them into the ring. Practising on equipment such as the punching bag, pull-up bar, dumbbells and treadmill, all award your boxer with Dexterity Exp.

GAMESWARRIOR VERDICT

Boxing League offers players a rewarding fighting game, one that takes time to master. However, the more matches you win and the more training you do, the better your chances of becoming the one true king of the ring!

GW RATING ★★★★★

MUSCLE LEGENDS

Here's your chance to flex and unleash your strength in the unstoppable Muscle Legends! Train your body to the peak of physical perfection, battle other players, gain new moves and level up to become a true fighting champion.

When you first start out in Muscle Legends, your character is pretty weak. It's only by working out, pumping iron and building up your strength that you'll be able to progress and take on other players who may be much tougher than they look!

Developer Scriptbloxian Studios has recently added Quests to the game, which require players to speak to other characters, complete tasks and earn rewards. The best players should have no problem finishing them all though!

As well as training and fighting, players really enjoy having their own epic pets, many of which can evolve over time. One strategy gamers use is to add pets to their collection using the crystals that appear in new arenas with tokens.

Top Muscle Legends take their time building up their characters' bodies and abilities before unleashing them in an arena. New players often find out the hard way what happens when they try to take on someone much bigger than themselves!

GAMESWARRIOR VERDICT

With great balance, training and battles, Muscle Legends is a really rewarding Roblox fighting game. With the right amount of workouts and fights, players will soon discover that they too can become one of the toughest brawlers in town!

RATING ★★★★★

HOURS

A fighting game with a twist, Hours lets players become one of 15 Hosts, each of which has a special set of abilities and can even control time. By facing off against endless waves of enemies, you'll become stronger and even more powerful!

Most players usually start off trying out the Very Easy setting in the game, to get to grips with how to play it. Gamers can also try their hand at Hourglass, an additional speedrunning mode that lets you set your own record times for battles.

One smart strategy some players use is to mix and match their time (or Tempo) powers to see what kinds of unique moves they can pull off. It's possible to stop time, go through time loops and even predict the future – a very useful ability!

Hours includes more than 30 challenging enemies and bosses, each of which will test a player's skills to the max. Gamers that can't take down their foes before the timer runs out get reset back to the start and lose any progress they've made.

GAMESWARRIOR VERDICT

With cool moves, great upgrades, tough enemies and a perfect learning curve, Hours is one of the most unique Roblox fighting games available. Players will challenge themselves to become better Hosts and to beat their previous scores and times.

GW RATING ★★★★★

THE STRONGEST BATTLEGROUNDS

With over 4.5 billion visits to date, The Strongest Battlegrounds is one of most popular Roblox fighting games ever. Train hard, take down your opponents and then level up to take on even tougher foes – this brawler has it all!

There are eight different characters to choose from in The Strongest Battlegrounds, with each having their own special abilities. However, players who want to add Wild Psychic to their line-up can only do so by getting the Early Access gamepass.

Each character has four main moves, which can be combined together to cause some serious damage to your enemies. All of the fighters also have an Ultimate move, which can be used by hitting opponents and filling up an onscreen bar.

As well as being able to master your own powers and fighting abilities, players also have the option to train others. That gives experienced gamers the chance to pass on what they're learned to noobs just starting out!

In addition to basic attack and the Ultimate, each character can block and dash. Some players are talented enough to use of all those abilities in a fight, ensuring that they always come out on top at the end of a fierce battle.

Battles take place in various arenas, with free-for-all fights breaking out as soon as you enter. One useful strategy to try out is to avoid all of the most powerful combatants at the start and let other players wear them down first!

The Strongest Battlegrounds was originally called Saitama Battlegrounds when it was launched by developer Yielding Arts in 2022. A lot of the characters were based on the anime, One-Punch Man, but that version has been deleted.

Some players choose to check out the The Strongest Battlegrounds Store to pick up handy items that can help them in the game. These include the Early Access gamepass, Special Cosmetics, Extra Emote Slots and a unique Kill Sound!

GAMESWARRIOR VERDICT

The Strongest Battlegrounds currently rules the roost when it comes to top Roblox fighting games. Although there are currently only eight characters to choose from, they're all worth mastering so that you can become a battling master!

GW RATING ★ ★ ★ ★ ★

SURVIVAL GAMING STRATEGIES

Although the actual locations for each Roblox survival experience can be very different, a lot of the basics are the same. By following the game's initial instructions, you'll soon learn what to do in order to stay alive and to keep progressing.

One good strategy some players use is to hold back and watch what happens to other gamers first. That's a smart way to tackle a survival game, as you can avoid losing your life by seeing how others tackle certain situations.

As with other Roblox games, levelling up as soon as possible can be a massive benefit. Reaching high levels as quickly as you can may seem like a bit of a grind, but it's the only way you'll stand a chance of making it through each stage.

If a survival game has its own store, then be sure to check it out. There might be handy extra items in there that can really help you complete each level, with some costing in-game currency and others requiring Robux for purchases.

Working as part of a team in many Roblox survival games is a strategy that many pro gamers use. By collaborating with others to complete goals, everyone benefits from any rewards, achievements and opportunities to level up.

GAMESWARRIOR SAYS

Roblox survival games offer all kinds of different experiences and may seem a little daunting at first. However, players who stay with the games and put in plenty of practise will soon discover just how good they are at making it through in one piece!

APOCALYPSE RISING 2

One of the best Roblox survival games available, Apocalypse Rising 2, tasks players with staying alive in a world full of zombies. That means a lot of grinding to get the best resources, weapons and vehicles, while keeping an eye out for the undead!

Fortunately, there are lots of abandoned buildings in each world that contain plenty of loot. Smart players know to head there as soon as the game begins to stock up on all of the essentials they can carry, before taking on any zombies.

One of the things many players really like about Apocalypse Rising 2 is that the game features random events that can really change what happens. That includes a helicopter crashing, boss fights and other surprises!

Gamers will also have their hands full with Apocalypse Rising 2. Not only do they have to watch out for the undead and useful items, but there are also enemy players out there that can cause you also plenty of trouble.

That's why many players choose to work together as a squad to survive for longer in Apocalypse Rising 2. This strategy is a really good idea, as long as gamers remember to communicate with each other so everyone knows what they're all doing.

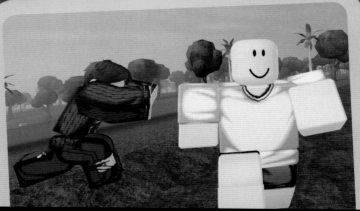

GAMESWARRIOR VERDICT

It may be the end of the world in Apocalypse Rising 2, but you'll have a blast with this ultimate Roblox survival experience. You might not last long the first time you play it, but stick with the game, level up and join with others to keep going.

GW RATING ★★★★☆

BEDWARS

In BedWars, players have to defend their area of the map from enemy attacks and see who can survive the longest. Defend your bed at all costs, because once it's gone, you won't be able to respawn and keep playing!

The good news is that there are plenty of weapons to choose from in BedWars, with more becoming available as you progress. Smart gamers know to gather resources and upgrades in order to access even better weapons later on.

One of the best strategies some players use is to join forces with others to form a squad. This is a great idea as a team of defenders will have a much better chance of keeping their bed in one piece than a lone warrior!

You can also do damage to other player's beds by attacking their bases. BedWars has more than 10 different game modes to try out, with many players choosing to go for the Lucky Block, SkyWars and Infected options.

GAMESWARRIOR VERDICT

With nearly nine billion visits to date, it's clear that BedWars is a real Roblox winner. This is one of the best experiences to tackle as a team, with strength in numbers usually proving the best way to survive each round intact!

RATING ★★★★★

SHARKBITE CLASSIC

You might not want to go swimming again after you've played SharkBite Classic! In this great survival game, you take on the role of either a mega-sized shark looking for its next lunch or as a human battling to survive with friends in a boat.

The good news for those taking on the role of a person is that there are all kinds of different weapons you can use to defend yourself. Top players hold on to any shark teeth they're rewarded at the end of each round and use them to buy the best stuff from the store!

If you choose to play as the shark, you'll get to swim around during each game and have to sneak up on the unsuspecting humans. One useful strategy is to take your time picking the boats apart one by one, so that you don't get hit by any weapons.

People that manage to successfully survive each round can then head to the in-game store to buy better boats and weapons, while shark players get to unlock even more huge predators, such as the massive prehistoric Mosasaurus!

GAMESWARRIOR VERDICT

SharkBite Classic is an absolute blast to play on your own or with friends. Working together as a team can be really rewarding, but becoming the monster shark and scaring everyone with sneak attacks it also tons of fun!

RATING ★★★★★

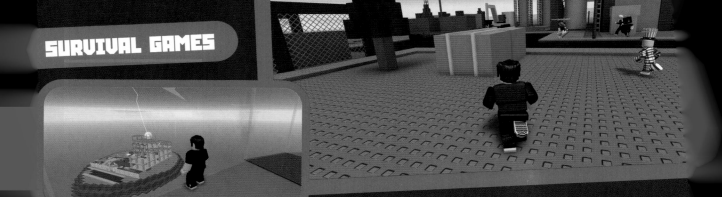

NATURAL DISASTER SURVIVAL

First unleashed all the way back in 2011, Natural Disaster Survival is not only one of the oldest Roblox games, but also one of the best. Do you have what it takes to battle your way through the elements and make it through to the next level?

There are currently 12 different kinds of disasters in the game, located in one of 22 preset maps. Players are spawned onto an elevated platform at the start of each round and then tasked with finding safety before the next disaster hits.

Those gamers who manage to survive the round then return back to the spawn tower before moving on to the next stage. Top players can get through all of the rounds without losing a life, as they always know the best places to head to!

One good strategy to know going into the game is that each type of disaster can be figured out by observing the weather before a round begins. For instance, dust appears before a sandstorm and a large wave pops up in the ocean before a tsunami.

Pro gamers usually head to the store before starting a game so that they can stock up on different items. The Green Balloon allows players to jump higher, the Red Apple heals damage and the Yellow Compass lets you choose the map.

Experienced players looking for more of a challenge tend to buy the Power-Up Machine. This device costs 100 Robux and can be used to combine multiple disasters into one round, giving top gamers a real run for their money!

A handy trick that some pro players use when their health has been depleted is to simply jump off the spawn tower. This is a good idea as it resets your health back up to 100% so that you can tackle the next disaster at full strength.

Another useful strategy that many gamers take advantage of is to never head to the highest spot in a level before disaster hits. That's smart thinking, as some of the dangerous weather will hit those taller locations first.

GAMESWARRIOR VERDICT

Natural Disaster Survival has been, and continues to be, a massive Roblox hit. Developer Stickmasterluke has created a really fun experience that pits people against the elements to see who will live to tell the tale and the results are totally amazing.

RATING ★★★★★

SPORTS GAMING STRATEGIES

If you're new to the world of sports games, then Roblox has you well and truly covered! Whether it's football, basketball, American football, dodgeball, golf, driving, hockey or tennis, there's an awesome experience for everyone.

Most of the best players usually pick a sport that they like in real life and then see just how good they are with a Roblox version. By spending a lot of time learning all about each experience and learning how to play well, you too can become a real pro!

A lot of Roblox sports games are best played as part of a team. By joining up with other gamers from around the world, you'll soon discover how to work together to take down your opponents and pick up tips from other players.

One good strategy some players try is to use items from a game's store or purchase upgrades to boost their characters. Those extra items can sometimes make a difference when it comes to winning or losing a match!

Don't expect to become a sporting superstar straight away. Top players know they have to put in a lot of work and game time to master their chosen Roblox sports game, but once they have they'll be able to call themselves real champions.

GAMESWARRIOR SAYS

Sports games are some of the most popular experiences in Roblox and it's easy to see why. With so many different sports on offer, there's always something new to discover and try, so get ready to hit the pitch, bash that ball and become a sporting superstar!

BASKETBALL PRO SIMULATOR

When it comes to a very different kind of sports game, then Basketball Pro Simulator is in a league of its own. The aim is to try and score as many hoops as you can from any distance using a variety of special balls.

One of the best Roblox basketball titles available, this experience allows players to earn coins and gems, which can then be used to buy upgrades for your character. There are also fun extras to buy such as skins, trails, goal effects and much more!

The main strategy most players use in Basketball Pro Simulator is to keep shooting hoops and earning coins. That's a good approach as the more cash you have, the better stuff you'll then be able to purchase to improve your overall game.

Developer LemonBread Studio is always adding regular updates to Basketball Pro Simulator, such as more unique worlds to try out. Players enjoy visiting the game all the time to discover what's new and what fun extras are now available.

Pro gamers know that coins also come in handy for upgrading the power available to their character. Once you've boosted your abilities, you'll be able to shoot further, add more speed and hit your target accurately!

GAMESWARRIOR VERDICT

If you've never played a Roblox basketball game, then Basketball Pro Simulator is definitely a great place to start. It's a really fun take on the sport and gives players plenty of modes, worlds, power-up, abilities and rewards. It's a slam dunk!

DODGEBALL!

One of players' all-time favourite Roblox games, Dodgeball! launched in 2015 and has had over 65 million views to date. Join a team, play with your friends, throw with plenty of accuracy and don't forget to dodge those balls!

Figuring out how to play Dodgeball! won't take you very long at all. At the start of every game, you have to join either the red or blue team and then select from a variety of different modes, such as Classic and Juggernaut.

In the main game, players have to throw balls at the opposition team and try to avoid getting hit themselves. If you get tagged four times in a row, then you have to sit out the rest of the game until the next round starts.

A good strategy some players use is to hang back slightly from the rest of the team and concentrate on accurate throwing. This is definitely a good idea as you can pick off any stragglers or sneaky opponents from a safe distance.

GAMESWARRIOR VERDICT

With fun modes and fast-paced action from the start, Dodgeball! is one of the most enjoyable Roblox games out there. Play solo or team up with your friends to form a squad and take on others, as you strive to become a true champion thrower!

RATING ★★★★★

GOAL KICK SIMULATOR

The idea behind Goal Kick Simulator is just that, take multiple shots at scoring and try to improve your accuracy over time. It may sound simple, but gamers often find themselves playing for hours as they try to better themselves!

As you may expect, each round starts with your player placing the ball on the goal spot and lining up their shot. There are various ways to change how you kick the ball and most players tend to go for speed over precision.

However, top gamers know that accuracy and speed combined are the keys to successfully putting the ball into he back of the net each time. That's why they put in plenty of time learning how to get the most out of Goal Kick Simulator's options.

Some of the game's mechanics are really fun and can give you all sorts of crazy objectives. For instance, scoring from the moon is hilarious and there are multiple chests to unlock that contain lots of different rewards, such as special balls.

GAMESWARRIOR VERDICT

Goal Kick Simulator takes a simple idea and works it into a must-play Roblox experience. This is definitely one solo game that you'll be playing for ages, as you slowly boost your skills and learn how to take the very best shots possible.

GW RATING ★★★★★

SUPER STRIKER LEAGUE

Super Striker League takes the most popular sport in the world and pushes it to the extreme! This is football like you've never seen it before, with two teams using power-ups and special abilities to take down their opponents.

One key reason why a lot of players like Super Striker League so much is that they're able to rise up the ranks of the game the more time they spend practising. Doing so then gives you access to more items and upgrades to really boost your squad!

Super Striker's Ranked Modes option is very popular too, with teams battling it out to score as many points as they can within a very tight time limit. Gamers like working together to beat the opposition and come out on top as true champions.

Players find that the three key abilities they need to keep an eye on during any matches are Power, Speed and Defense, while pros know that mastering and combining all three will lead to victory each and every time.

Gamers also soon learn that they need to understand all about kicking, tackling, stamina and dodging to beat other players. Fortunately, there's a handy Supercharge bar that builds up during matches that can then be used to power up your character for a short time!

Pro players have no problem getting the ball past the goalkeeper every single time. The lower the goalie's stamina is, the slower they'll react to kicks. A lot of gamers also try to lure the goalkeeper away from their area, then sneak round the back to score.

There are lots of different items that can be obtained in Super Striker League, many of which will give you the edge on the pitch. These include Strikez Cola, Bomb, Giant Boulder and Triple Boulder, plus the rare Invincibility Star.

Another reason lots of players keep coming back to Super Striker League is for regular events. Egg Hunt 2000, RB Battles Season 2 and Metaverse Champions all rewarded gamers with exclusive items that can't be found anywhere else!

GAMESWARRIOR VERDICT

Whether in solo mode or as part of team, you're definitely going to want to play Super Striker League. The fact that it's football with an edge makes it even more enjoyable and some of the power-ups and abilities are just so much fun!

ULTIMATE ROBLOX QUIZ ANSWERS

1 **Which 2024 metaverse event involved 100 different Roblox games?**
The Hunt: First Edition

2 **What's the Max Level that you can reach in RPG Simulator?**
1,401

3 **How many visits has Speed Run 4 had to date?**
The Hunt: First Edition

4 **What's the maximum number of players that can take part in Hide and Seek Extreme?**
13

5 **Which Roblox game has added cute pet patients on its Sky Floor?**
Hospital Tycoon

6 **What's the name of the developer behind Bee Swarm Simulator?**
Onett

7 **What was the original title of The Strongest Battlegrounds?**
Saitama Battlegrounds

8 **Which survival game lets you unlock and play as a prehistoric Mosasaurus?**
SharkBite Classic

9 **What are the names of the two coloured teams in Dodgeball!?**
Red and Blue

10 **Which sportswear brand added virtual pop-up shops in Roblox in 2024?**
adidas

11 **What do you get when you verify your Roblox account?**
A free item

12 **What's the name of the Roblox paid-for subscription service?**
Roblox Premium

13 **Which Roblox RPG was inspired by the Sword Art Online anime?**
Swordburst 2

14 **What's the name of the mini-boss in Soul War?**
WEEGEE

15 **How many different stages are currently in Cotton Obby!?**
55

16 **What creature do you start out as in Little World?**
Ladybug

17 **Which simulator game includes over 1,000 pets?**
Pet Simulator X

18 **How many new skill moves can you unlock in Boxing League?**
14

19 **In which year did Natural Disaster Survival launch?**
2011

20 **Which sports game lets you score a goal from the moon?**
Goal Kick Simulator